STAR WARS REBELS™

SABINE'S ART ATTACK

ADAPTED BY JENNIFER HEDDLE

BASED ON THE EPISODE "ART ATTACK,"
WRITTEN BY GREG WEISMAN

Disney
LUCASFILM
PRESS

LOS ANGELES • NEW YORK

Published by Disney • Lucasfilm Press, an imprint of Disney Book Group. No part of this book
may be reproduced or transmitted in any form or by any means, electronic or mechanical,
including photocopying, recording, or by any information storage and retrieval system, without
written permission from the publisher. For information address Disney • Lucasfilm Press, 1101
Flower Street, Glendale, California 91201.

Printed in the United States of America

First Edition, January 2015 10 9 8 7 6 5 4 3 2 1

Library of Congress Control Number: 2014947444

G658-7729-4-14325

ISBN 978-1-4847-0491-2

SUSTAINABLE
FORESTRY
INITIATIVE

Certified Chain of Custody
Promoting Sustainable Forestry

www.sfiprogram.org
SFI-01415
The SFI label applies to the text stock

Visit the official *Star Wars* website at: www.starwars.com

Meet Sabine.

She loves to paint.

She is an artist.

She is also a rebel.
She fights for what is right.

One night, Sabine ran
through Lothal.
She had to hide from
the troopers.

The troopers were from the
Empire.
Sabine did not like troopers.

Sabine found a lot of TIE
fighters.
The TIE fighters belonged
to the Empire.

Sabine took out her spray
can. She began to paint.
Two troopers found her.

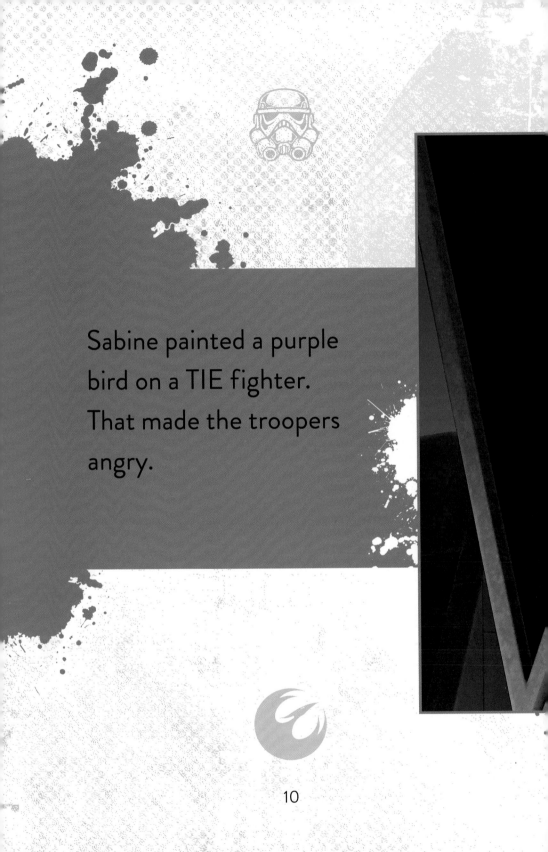

Sabine painted a purple
bird on a TIE fighter.
That made the troopers
angry.

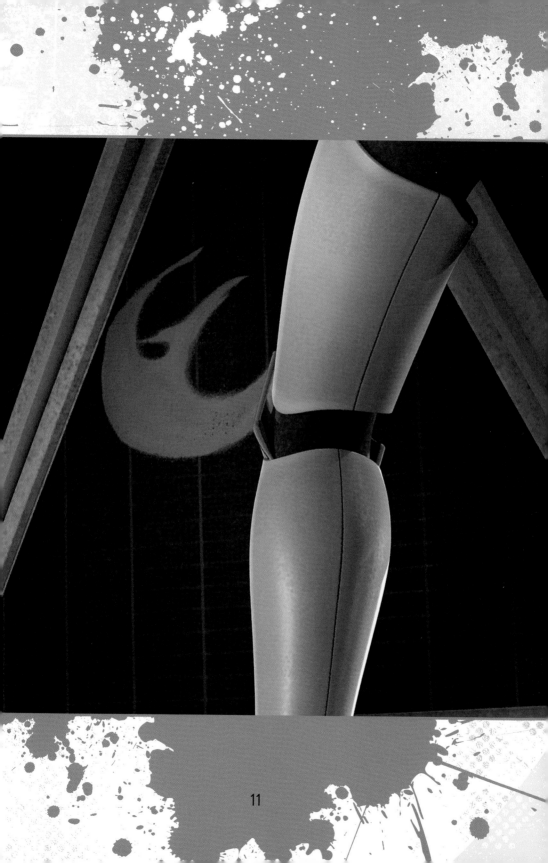

They told Sabine to stop.
They said they would shoot.
Sabine said, "Okay. Shoot!"

The troopers were confused.
Sabine ran away.

Sabine was good at
hiding. She was also
very fast.

The troopers tried to shoot her.
They always missed.

Sabine made fun of the
troopers.
She said they needed
target practice.

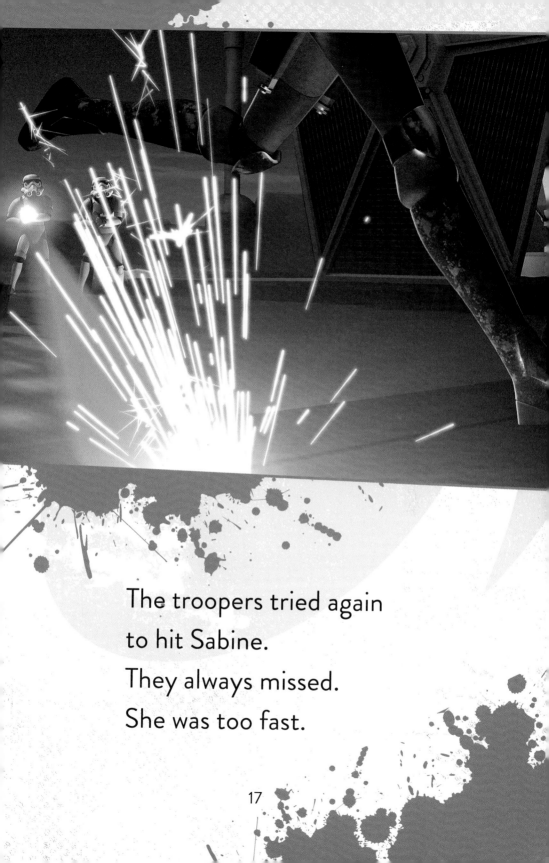

The troopers tried again
to hit Sabine.
They always missed.
She was too fast.

Sabine went back to her
painting.
It needed something
extra special.

Then a trooper found
her!
Sabine was in trouble!

Sabine kicked the
trooper in the leg.
The trooper fell.
Sabine ran away.

The other troopers looked
for Sabine.
They could not find her.

They looked at the painting
of the bird.
They saw something extra
special.

Sabine had added a bomb
to the painting!
Uh-oh!

Boom! The bomb went off.
The troopers fell over.
But not Sabine!
She was too fast.

Sabine stopped.

She took off her helmet.

She looked back.

She liked what she saw.